ANTLERS FOREVER!

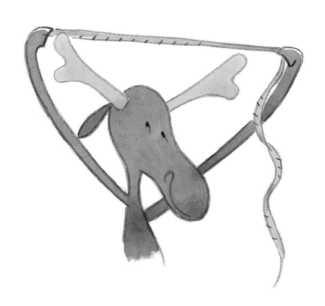

written by FRANCES BLOXAM
illustrated by JIM SOLLERS

■ DOWN EAST BOOKS ■

DOWN EAST BOOKS / ROCKPORT, MAINE

Book orders: 1-800-766-1670

For Big Dog

And our children

And our children's children

With love

When young Orville Anderson Tarkington Moose
awoke one bright morning, his antlers were loose.

"Oh, dear!" cried poor Orville. "A terrible thing!
I've worked on these antlers since early last spring!
Now winter is coming, and what shall I do
without my fine antlers? Oh, boo hoo hoo hoooo!

"I've polished them daily and kept them quite strong.
Now, what in the world do you think has gone wrong?

"It's Vitamin M!
That's the thing I must lack.
You get that from beezels,
and those grow out back.
I really hate beezels—
they're stringy and tough—
but losing your antlers
is serious stuff!"

So Orville ate beezels,
ate beezels galore,
until he was full,
then he burped and ate more!

"I'm so full of beezels, I'll sit down right here."
He sat—and one antler slid over his ear!
"How dreadful!" groaned Orville. "This really is foul!
I need good advice, so I'll go talk to Owl."

(Because of his eyes and the calm way he sits
Owl looks like a bird with remarkable wits.)

He walked with great care down the path to Owl's tree.
He knocked and he waved and then called out, "It's me!
I have a big problem—my antlers go flop!
If they aren't fixed soon, I'm afraid they will drop!"

Owl blinked his large eyes, and he curled his strong toes.
Just what he was thinking of, nobody knows.

"Young Orville," said Owl, "I'd have thought that you knew
that antlers like yours are held on by a screw.
Your screw has come loose, as screws sometimes will do.
(This makes you screw loose—hee ho ho, hah hoooo!)

"To fix them is simple: we'll screw them back in.
I'll hold them in place while you turn 'round and spin."
"Oh, thank you!" said Orville. "You're so very kind.
Grab hold of my antlers—we'll give them a wind!"

With Owl holding on, Orville started to spin.
There was screeching and flapping—a terrible din!
When finally they quit, Orville crashed in a heap,
and Owl was too tired to make even a peep.

They waited a minute, till all the dust cleared,
and then Orville saw it was just as he'd feared . . .

His antlers were off! There they lay on the ground!
Poor Orville was stunned. He could not make a sound.

Then . . .

He threw back his head and he cried and he howled.
He wept and he snorted and bellowed and yowled!

A big voice then called out, "Come, come, my sad fellow!
I was miles away, but I heard every bellow.
Explain your loud cries. They're upsetting us all."
When Orville looked up, he saw *this* moose was tall!

A moose large and broad, with a beautiful beard.
"Oh, sir!" said young Orville. "It's just as I feared.
I just could not save them! My antlers fell off!
It's terribly sad! Now my friends will all scoff!"

Said Big Moose, "What nonsense! It's clear you don't know
that moose shed their antlers so new ones can grow.
You must wait till spring, when new antlers will sprout.
And they'll be much bigger, of that have no doubt.
They'll also be heavy, and that's why it's best
that antlers fall off, so our heads get a rest.

"It's ANTLERS FOREVER! A new pair each spring!
Isn't being a moose just a marvelous thing?
Goodbye, Orville Anderson Tarkington Moose.
I'll soon look like you, 'cause *my* antlers are loose!"

And that is the story of Orville, the moose,
who learned not to fret when his antlers got loose!

Learn About Antlers...

When do moose get their antlers?

Antlers begin to grow when a moose is about a year old. By the time he is eighteen months old (in September or October), a young moose will have small, spiky antlers.

When do they grow those big, fancy antlers?

Large antlers with many prongs come as the moose grows older. Food is as important as age, though. A moose has to have plenty of good food to grow large antlers.

7 ft.

How big can the antlers grow?

On a healthy older moose that gets plenty of food, the antlers can be as large as seven feet across and weigh from thirty-five to forty-four pounds. The largest moose antler ever found weighed seventy-nine pounds!

Are both antlers exactly the same?

Yes, usually they are a matched pair. They are like your hands—a right and a left. Sometimes an injury or poor food will cause one antler to look a little different from the other.

What happens to the shed antlers?

They are nibbled on by mice, porcupines, and rabbits. What is left gradually crumbles into the soil. The little creatures that nibble get good vitamins and minerals from the dropped antlers.

Why don't the antlers just stay on all the time?

It is easier for a moose to get through the winter without having to carry those huge antlers around. He needs less to eat, and he can move more quickly and easily.

Does it hurt when they come off?
No, although the spot where the antler used to be looks red for a while.

When do moose shed their antlers?
Antlers fall off sometime between mid-December and January. Sometimes both antlers fall off at once, but usually moose drop their antlers one at a time. It must feel odd to walk around with one antler!

What about the new antlers?
The new antlers grow exactly where the old ones used to be. They first begin to show in April, and they grow *very* fast. While they are growing, they are covered with a fuzzy skin called velvet. When the antlers reach full-size, in August, the velvet dries up. Then the moose rubs his antlers back and forth in bushes and low trees to get the velvet off. It seems to itch. The new antlers are very hard and strong.

Why don't cow moose have antlers?
They use their energy in other ways. Instead of growing antlers, they are busy bearing and raising their calves. Moose calves are helpless when they are first born, and their mothers have to protect them at all times. Even though a mother moose does not have antlers, she is a fierce warrior when she is defending her calf!

Do all moose have antlers?
No, only bull moose (the males) grow antlers. Females (called cows) never have them.

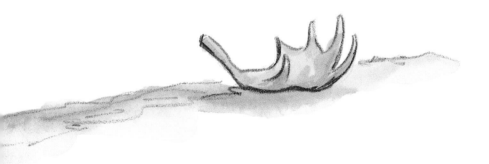

Why do moose have antlers at all?
Antlers make a bull moose look impressive. A fine set of antlers shows a cow moose that the bull is strong and healthy and would make a good mate. Bull moose also use their antlers to compete with each other for mates. Sometimes they actually use their antlers to fight, but most of the time the contest is settled with just antler-shaking and bellowing. After the fall mating season is finished, the male moose hang around together, eat a lot, and do some friendly antler-sparring until they finally shed their antlers for the winter.